STEAMTEAM 5 CHRONICLES

EVELYN ENGINEER AND THE LIGHTNING TREASURE

GREG HELMSTETTER
PAMELA METIVIER

MONSOON PUBLISHING

Written by Greg Helmstetter & Pamela Metivier

Illustrated by Greg Helmstetter

Printed in the U.S.A.

CONTENTS

OTHER STEAMTEAM 5 BOOKS

STEAMTeam 5 Book 1: The Beginning

STEAMTeam 5 Book 2: Mystery at Makerspace

STEAMTeam 5 Chronicles: Mystery of the Haunted Cider Mill

FREE EBOOK

To receive a free .PDF of *STEAMTeam 5 Chronicles: Mystery of the Haunted Cider Mill,* send an email to **info@steamteam5.com.**

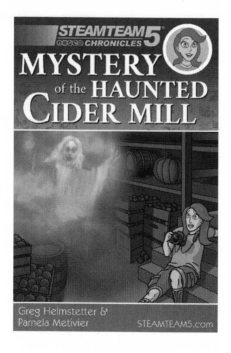

THE GRIPPERATOR

The sun had barely risen, and Evelyn was already busy working on a project in her machine shop.

The machine shop was where she worked on her engineering projects—the place where she cut, shaped, drilled, and assembled her inventions.

Her parents parked one of their cars in the driveway to give Evelyn a large portion of the garage to use for her machine shop, and she made good use of it almost every day.

On this particular day, she was working on her newest invention. As was always the case, Evelyn liked to keep her new inventions secret until they were ready for the "big reveal."

As she tinkered away, the doorbell rang—three times in a row.

"Grandma!" she exclaimed.

Evelyn's great-grandmother—Grandma Helen—always rang the doorbell three times in a row when she dropped by for a visit. She called it her "special calling card."

Evelyn threw a sheet over her secret project and raced into the house to greet her.

"Grandma!" Evelyn cried out, wrapping her arms around her grandmother with such force she nearly knocked her over.

"Be careful," her mother warned.

"Sorry Grandma," Evelyn winced.

Grandma Helen laughed. She appreciated Evelyn's enthusiasm.

Evelyn noticed she was pulling a large suitcase.

"Are you staying with us?" Evelyn asked excitedly.

"No," Grandma Helen replied. She lived in a retirement community just a few miles away, so she didn't spend the night very often.

"I brought you a treat," her grandmother said with a wink.

"This was the best way to cart it over here," she added, pushing the suitcase toward Evelyn.

"Yay!" Evelyn rejoiced, clapping her hands. "I love your treats!"

Grandma Helen always brought the best treats. Evelyn's other grandmother brought candy, clothes, and other wonderful items when she visited from Chicago, which she loved. But Grandma Helen usually brought old treasures she had tucked away from her younger, adventurous days.

"Go, ahead! Open it!" Grandma Helen insisted.

Evelyn rolled the suitcase to the living room and opened it up.

The suitcase contained a contraption unlike anything Evelyn had ever seen before.

Evelyn examined the item closely. It comprised several metal panels, connected by hinges. There was a control box on it and a long black cord.

"Is this an old ironing board?" Evelyn guessed.

"Close!" Grandma Helen replied, beaming with pride.

"Obviously, it's an appliance of some kind," Evelyn mumbled.

Grandma Helen smiled. Grandma Helen and Evelyn had an unspoken agreement that they never explained an invention until the other person was done guessing.

After several more incorrect—but close—guesses, Evelyn announced, "I give up!"

"It's one of my very first inventions—I think I completed it in 1953," Grandma began.

"It's an electronic fitted sheet folder!" Grandma Helen revealed.

Evelyn's mouth dropped open. This was the first time she'd heard about this invention.

"One of my least favorite household tasks has always been folding laundry," Grandma Helen explained. "And folding fitted sheets always tried my patience. Who has time for that? I decided long ago that fitted sheets were a problem just begging for a solution."

"Agree!" said Evelyn's father. He had been eavesdropping from across the room.

"Let's go to your workshop and I'll show you how it works!" Grandma Helen suggested.

"I'll grab a sheet!" Evelyn exclaimed.

Five minutes later, Grandma Helen and Evelyn disappeared into the garage with a bed sheet in tow.

Grandma Helen rested the large metal folding board onto the workspace and tucked all four ends of a twin-sized fitted bed sheet into an opening on each corner of the board.

She plugged the power cord into the wall and then pushed the "Start" button on the side of the board. The top left corner of the board began to move, folding the sheet in half vertically.

Next, the lower right corner of the folding board moved, folding the sheet once again—this time horizontally.

One by one, the other sections of the folding board performed a unique movement until the sheet was folded into a perfect square.

"Survival of the fitted," Grandma Helen said to herself, chuckling.

Evelyn cackled in delight.

Grandma Helen noticed the sheet wasn't as perfectly folded as she remembered they used to be.

"It's loosened up over time. Let's tighten up the hinges a bit," she suggested.

"No problem," Evelyn said as she reached into one of the drawers on her workbench.

She patted her hand around inside the drawer.

"Come on, Gripperator, where are you?" said Evelyn.

The Gripperator, a one-size-fits-all wrench that she had bought off a TV infomercial, was Evelyn's favorite wrench.

"Where are you?" she repeated. Evelyn pulled the drawer all the way out and searched feverishly for her go-to tool.

But the Gripperator wasn't in there.

"Huh," Evelyn said. She was confused. She always left the Gripperator in the top drawer of her bench when she wasn't using it. In fact, she had just used it the night before.

Evelyn spent the next several minutes looking everywhere in her workshop for the wrench. Much to her dismay, her search was fruitless. The only thing she'd found was a regular crescent wrench. She slid the crescent wrench into her back pocket.

"I can't find my Gripperator," Evelyn said with a loud sigh.

"How about if we take a short break? I could use a cool glass of water," Grandma Helen suggested.

Grandma Helen knew it always helped Evelyn deal with frustrating things when she took a short water break.

Evelyn dragged herself into the house, and Grandma Helen followed behind her.

Evelyn grabbed two glasses from the cupboard and began to fill them with water from the refrigerator. Grandma Helen sat on a chair nearby.

Suddenly, Evelyn's dog Beulah appeared out of nowhere. (Anytime anyone went near the fridge, Beulah appeared within seconds.)

Beulah sat politely at Evelyn's feet and looked up to her, wagging her tail.

"Hi Beulah," Evelyn said.

Beulah licked her chops in response.

"Hey, Beulah..." Evelyn started. "Have you seen my Gripperator?"

Beulah cocked her head slightly.

Evelyn pulled the regular crescent out of her back pocket. "It looks kinda like this," she explained.

Beulah's tail stopped wagging, and she looked down at the floor.

"Beu...lah?" Evelyn asked slowly.

Suddenly, Beulah barked and began wagging her tail vigorously. Then she darted out the doggy door leading to the backyard.

"Oh, please tell me you didn't!" Evelyn moaned, as she ran after Beulah into the backyard. Grandma Helen stayed behind to enjoy her glass of water.

Evelyn stood on the patio as Beulah darted around the backyard, barking loudly.

"Beulah," you're going to wake up the whole neighborhood," Evelyn whispered sternly.

Beulah didn't seem to mind if the neighbors heard her. She was excited to demonstrate her helpfulness to Evelyn.

Beulah ran over to a mound of dirt and sat down next to it. Her tail thumped against the ground with gusto.

Evelyn winced, then walked over to the mound. She wasn't happy that Beulah buried the wrench, but all would be forgiven if the dog could help her find it.

Evelyn dug into the ground with her bare hands, removing fistfuls of dirt, piling it to the side of the hole.

After several minutes of digging, Evelyn felt something hard.

She was ecstatic! She pulled the object out of the dirt and held it up to get a close look.

"A bone," Evelyn sighed. She showed the bone to Beulah.

"It's about the size of a wrench, and it's kind of shaped like a wrench, but it's just a bone," she said.

Beulah barked and sprang up onto all four legs. Without warning, she ran over to another mound of dirt about 20 feet away and started thumping her tail excitedly.

Once again, Evelyn followed Beulah and began digging.

And, once again, Evelyn found a bone.

"Another bone," Evelyn reported, disappointed.

Beulah wagged her tail in excitement. She continued running all over the yard, from one mound to another.

Evelyn began to approach another mound of dirt and then suddenly stopped in her tracks.

She gazed at the sight of a yard full of mounds of dirt—dozens, maybe a hundred—scattered all around her.

Beulah had mistakenly buried the wrench, but now the poor little pup couldn't remember where she buried it.

Evelyn thought for a moment, the way she always did when she was about to start doing something hard. Evelyn always tried to find a better way.

"Instead of digging up every hole," Evelyn said, "maybe we can be a little smarter."

"The wrench is made of metal, so I should be able to find it using a metal detector!"

Evelyn didn't have a metal detector, but that didn't matter.

After all, she was an engineer. She would do what she always does. She would build one.

2

BURIED TREASURES

"Grandma!" Evelyn said loudly as she entered the kitchen. "Want to help me with a new project?"

"Oh, I'd love to, darling," Grandma Helen replied, "but I have yoga class at the center in 30 minutes—in fact, I should be going."

Evelyn gave Grandma Helen a quick kiss and retreated to her machine shop with a single plan in mind: Building a metal detector.

"First things first," Evelyn reminded herself. "Research how metal detectors work."

She pulled her tablet out of her backpack and began

searching the Internet to learn everything she could about the different types of detector technology.

When she was done with her research, Evelyn sketched a design.

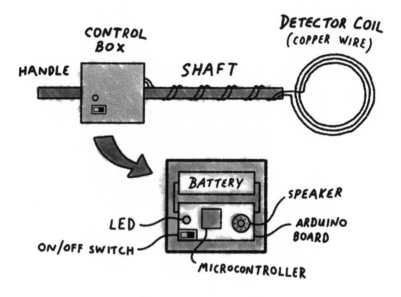

"I'll need a control box, a shaft, and a search coil," she said to herself as she sketched out the main components.

"There we go," she said confidently. "Now I have a plan."

Evelyn was refining her sketch when the door to the house swung open.

"Lunch is ready!" her mother announced.

Evelyn dropped her pencil and hurried into the house. She was hungry from all the digging and designing.

Evelyn slid onto a stool at the kitchen counter and began devouring a sandwich.

"Whatchya working on?" Evelyn's mom asked from the other side of the counter.

"Well, I was going to work on Grandma's sheet-folding invention, but Beulah buried my wrench somewhere in the backyard, so now I'm working on a metal detector to find it," Evelyn answered, matter-of-factly.

Evelyn's mother glanced outside the kitchen window into the backyard.

"Ah. That explains the holes," her mother replied.

"Yep," said Evelyn.

Just then, Evelyn's father joined them in the kitchen. He pulled his headphones out of his ears and greeted Evelyn.

"You've been busy today!" he said.

"She's building a metal detector," Evelyn's mother explained.

"Ah. That explains the holes," her father replied.

Evelyn finished the last bite of her sandwich. "Be right back!" she announced, as she disappeared into the garage. She returned a moment later with her drawing.

"Here's the plan," she said, as she lay her sketch on the countertop.

Both of her parents leaned in to take a closer look.

"Looks like a metal detector," her mother said.

"Yes, it does," her father agreed. "What's your plan for building it?"

"First, I'm going to scrounge for parts," Evelyn replied, grinning ear to ear.

Her parents looked at each other knowingly. Parental pride tinged with fear.

"Just remember…" her mother started.

"Ask before taking anything apart that already works," Evelyn said, finishing her mother's standard warning.

They all chuckled. Evelyn was famous for "borrowing" parts from household appliances.

The doorbell rang.

Evelyn suddenly remembered that her friend, Ariana, was coming over.

Ariana was a fantastic artist. She always had a way of making Evelyn's inventions more "user friendly." This was one of Ariana's superpowers. Evelyn could make things that solved problems, and Ariana could make those things easy or fun to use. Together, the two girls made a great team.

Evelyn jogged to the front door to greet her friend.

"Ariana!" she proclaimed as she opened the front door. Ariana smiled.

"I need your help!" Evelyn said. "I'll explain. Come on in!"

Evelyn grabbed her drawing and headed into the garage with Ariana.

From inside the house, Evelyn's parents could hear her and Ariana sifting through the garage in their search for parts for the new metal detector.

As Ariana and Evelyn rummaged through the garage, Ariana found an old yard trimmer that hadn't been used for years. She handed it to Evelyn. "Would this help?" asked Ariana.

"Absolutely!" replied Evelyn. "This will make a perfect shaft." Evelyn took the yard trimmer from Ariana's hands and examined it.

She placed the yard trimmer on the work table. "Shaft. Check!"

Ariana took a peek behind a large piece of plywood leaning against the garage wall.

"Careful," Evelyn warned. "There's a boobytrap behind there."

"A boobytrap?" Ariana asked.

"Let's just say Cartwright and I are on good terms—for now," Evelyn replied.

Ariana laughed. Cartwright was the neighborhood raccoon who had a bad habit of stealing Beulah's toys from the backyard. Evelyn had made a boobytrap to catch and release Cartwright, and she had used it at least three times over the past month. Thankfully, Cartwright now appeared to be on a break from her mischief-making.

"What's all this stuff?" Ariana asked as she opened a large plastic tub.

"Scuba stuff," Evelyn answered. "It's no use for this project."

"Gotcha," Ariana said, continuing to search the garage for any parts that might help them build the metal detector.

"What about the control box?" Ariana asked.

"Ah, yes!" Evelyn replied.

Evelyn pulled a plastic storage box off a shelf near her desk. She opened the box to peruse the contents.

The storage box had 18 small compartments. Each compartment contained a different type of electronic component.

Ariana picked up one of the components. "What's this?" she asked. "It looks like a bug."

"That's an integrated circuit," Evelyn answered. "We don't need one of those," she said, as she took the component from Ariana and returned it to the storage box.

"Instead, we'll use this Arduino board," she said, gently placing a small, blue circuit board onto the table. "It will be the brains of our detector. We'll attach components to it. A buzzer and LED—light emitting diode—to alert us when it senses metal."

"We need a nine-volt battery for power," Evelyn explained, as she picked one out of the box and stood it up on the table.

"And, we'll need to control the electricity," she added, picking out components from two separate compartments and placing them on the table. "These are resistors. They restrict the flow of the current in the circuit so our little parts don't get fried."

"Interesting," Ariana said, nodding.

"And a 10nF capacitor to store energy, of course," Evelyn added.

"Of course!" Ariana said, grinning.

Evelyn realized Ariana was teasing her, and she laughed along.

"We also need some copper coil and jumper wire," Evelyn said, as she pulled out two rolls of wire from her storage box.

"The coil and capacitor will be used to detect the metal," Evelyn explained.

"We'll need to cut the wire," said Evelyn as she reached into a drawer and removed a pair of wire cutters.

"Let's see. What else?..." Evelyn mumbled. She tapped her fingers on the table. "There's something I'm missing..."

"The thingy that holds the coil?" Ariana asked.

"Yes!" Evelyn cheered. "The search head... thank you!"

Evelyn lifted up the yard trimmer and held it in her hand. "I'll store the control in the motor housing," she explained. Ariana nodded in agreement.

"I bet I can replace this trimmer head with a search head," Evelyn said. "I need something round and flat, like a plate," Evelyn said, clicking her tongue.

They were both quiet for a moment. Evelyn scanned her work table. She spotted a compact disc under a glass of water.

"That's it!" Evelyn announced, pointing at the CD.

"A coaster?" Ariana asked. "Oh, wait. That's a disc! I get it! You can use it to support a wire coil!"

"Exactly!" Evelyn replied. "Let's go inside and find another disc. I'll sandwich the coil between two discs to protect it."

Into the house they went.

Evelyn and Ariana were searching through a desk in the living room when Evelyn's mother entered the room.

"Are you really looking for metal detector parts in there?" her mother asked.

"Yes," Evelyn replied, continuing her search.

"Voila!" Evelyn announced, as she removed a small stack of music CDs. She took one CD off the top of the stack. "We need another disc!"

"Hold on!" her mother called out as she approached them. "Which one is that?" she asked.

Evelyn read the words on the CD: "*Disintegration* by—" Evelyn began.

"Oh, no!" her mother blurted as she gently removed the CD from Evelyn's hands. "Not this one. It's my favorite."

Evelyn grinned and grabbed the next CD on the stack, showing her mother the label.

"Oh, that one's fine," her mother said.

Evelyn slipped the CD into her back pocket and headed to the garage.

"It's getting dark," Ariana said. "I'd better be getting home."

"Oh, bummer," Evelyn replied. "This day really flew by."

Ariana and Evelyn said their good-byes, then Evelyn disappeared into the garage to assemble her metal detector.

3

DETECTOROSA 850

*E*velyn reviewed her diagram for the metal detector one more time while she checked off her list of components she needed to build it.

"Looks like I'm ready!" she said, as she put on her safety goggles.

First, she began building the control box. It would be the "brain" of the metal detector. It's a plastic box that holds the components that control how the device works—in this case, using an electrical current to identify metal and notify the user with a flashing light and a "beep." Without the control box, the metal detector would just be a fancy stick.

Beulah sat nearby, watching intently.

"I'll set up the power supply," Evelyn explained to Beulah. Evelyn always explained what she was doing to her little canine "assistant." Thinking out loud helped her organize her thoughts and avoid making mistakes.

"I'll need this battery, LED with built-in resistor, power switch, and voltage regulator," she continued.

She moved the pieces into a pile, then turned on a soldering iron, hot glue gun, and smoke absorber fan that were plugged in nearby.

She took her time adding the battery pack and other components to the Arduino board.

"The buzzer and LED light will alert us when metal is detected," she explained to Beulah as she added those parts.

For the next step, Evelyn needed to connect the Arduino to her computer so she could upload computer code to it. The control box requires these instructions in order to know what to do when it encounters metal.

"Ta-da!" Evelyn announced several minutes later, showing her completed control box to Beulah.

Beulah wagged her tail.

"Next up is the search coil assembly!" Evelyn explained.

She spent the next twenty minutes winding several feet of copper transmitter into a coil. She sandwiched the coil between the two compact discs to hold them in place. She then taped everything together.

"Now, to assemble everything," Evelyn said to Beulah. This time, Beulah didn't wag her tail. She was sound asleep.

Evelyn looked at the trimmer's plastic guard. "Strictly speaking, we won't need this. But I kind of like it. Besides, it will protect the search head. I think I'll leave it on."

Evelyn connected the search head to the end of the shaft, beneath the plastic guard. She then wound copper wire up the shaft, to the handle.

Then, she opened the plastic housing on the handle of the yard trimmer and removed the motor inside of it. "I'll probably need this someday," she said, as she placed the motor on a shelf full of spare parts.

She measured and cut a hole into the side of the trimmer's plastic motor housing using a rotary tool. She then gently placed her new control box inside the hole.

"Fits perfectly!" she proclaimed.

She connected all of the components together and tested everything.

Evelyn took a step back to behold her new metal detector.

"I call this the Detectorosa 750!" she announced to Beulah, who was still sound asleep.

Evelyn glanced down at her watch. "Yikes! It's already 9:15!"

"It'll be too dark to use this today," she moaned. "But I don't want to wait until morning to try it out."

"Oh, wait," she murmured to herself.

Evelyn opened the top drawer in her desk and pulled out a small flashlight. Within minutes, she had mounted the flashlight to the shaft.

"Behold, the new and improved, *night-time* metal detector... the Detectorosa 850!"

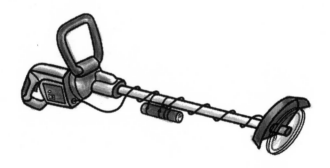

Beulah, who was snoring loudly by now, didn't even twitch.

"Beulah, wake up!" Evelyn commanded. "Game on!"

Beulah looked up groggily and followed Evelyn outside. The dog burst into action when she realized they were about to resume their hunt! Only this time, they would be using the Detectorosa 850. Beulah barked with excitement!

"Metal detection is based upon the principles of electromagnetic induction," Evelyn explained as they walked from one mound to another.

"When electricity flows from our battery, down through the coil on our metal detector, it creates a magnetic field around the search head," Evelyn continued.

"If I move the detector over a metal object, that field generates electrical activity in the metal."

"And the metal sends a signal back which basically says, 'Hey, I'm metal.'"

Beulah wasn't really listening. She was having too much fun guiding Evelyn to all of the mounds she had created.

As Beulah led the way from mound to mound, Evelyn slowly waved the metal detector above each one, listening for any indication of metal buried below.

Suddenly, there was a gust of wind, and a branch from one of the trees above them cracked.

"Whoa!" shouted Evelyn.

A bolt of lightning lit up the dark sky in the distance. Evelyn slowly started counting, "One Mississippi, two Mississippi, three Mississippi, four Mississippi..."

When she reached "twenty-five Mississippi," a rumbling sound startled Evelyn and sent Beulah cowering under a nearby tree.

"It's okay, Beulah," Evelyn said as she walked over to comfort Beulah. "That lightning is still pretty far away. Light travels faster than sound."

"After you see a flash of lightning, count the number of seconds until you hear the thunder. For every five seconds you count, the lightning is one mile away."

"I counted to twenty-five, so that means the storm is five miles away," Evelyn explained.

"We should go inside soon," she sighed. "But let's try a couple more spots first."

Evelyn and Beulah continued their search for the Gripperator. As they approached the next mound, Evelyn waved the metal detector slowly above it. The Detectorosa 850 let out a loud "BEEP!"

"Booyah!" Evelyn called out. She dropped down onto her knees and began digging. Beulah joined in, wagging her tail as she flung dirt behind her.

Beulah's head disappeared into the ground below and, about five seconds later, she reappeared with the Gripperator hanging out of her mouth.

"Good girl!" Evelyn cheered. She took the Gripperator out of Beulah's mouth.

Beulah's head was covered in dirt.

"Oh, Beulah," Evelyn laughed as she brushed the dirt away from her eyes.

Lightning flashed in the sky again. Evelyn stopped to count to herself. This time, the lightning was followed by a loud crack of thunder fifteen seconds later.

"The storm is getting closer," Evelyn warned. "It's now three miles away."

"Let's head inside Beulah," Evelyn said. "In the morning, we can refill all these holes we dug today."

Beulah whimpered. She was having so much fun playing in the dirt.

"Sorry pup, but we really need to get indoors," Evelyn explained, as she looked up at the sky. The wind had really picked up and began to make loud whooshing sounds as the treetops swayed back and forth.

She and Beulah made their way into the house and closed the door behind them.

Little did Evelyn or Beulah know, this was no ordinary storm heading straight at them.

4

THE STORM OF THE CENTURY

Seconds after Evelyn and Beulah closed the door behind themselves, rain began to fall. Gentle drops at first, then a steady flow, and then rain poured like buckets!

"Looks like we're in for quite a storm tonight," said Evelyn's dad, as he watched the news. "Maybe the biggest one in years."

Just then, thunder cracked, so loud it shook the house. Beulah barked and ran under the coffee table.

"Don't worry, pup," said Evelyn, as she sat down next to Beulah and scratched behind her ears. "It's just a little rain." Beulah came out of hiding and lay her head on Evelyn's lap, peeking anxiously at the windows.

LATER THAT NIGHT, EVELYN CLIMBED INTO BED WITH A BOOK. Her room was dark, except for a tiny book light Evelyn used to read before bed.

The pouring rain, howling wind, and occasional clap of thunder hadn't let up for a moment. It was bigger than any storm Evelyn had ever seen.

"Beulah," Evelyn whispered loudly as she lay in bed.

Normally, Beulah would hop onto the bed when her name was called. But, that night, she didn't.

Evelyn leaned over the side of her bed and looked underneath it. Her eyes met Beulah's. Poor Beulah was still frightened by the storm, and it was clear she wasn't interested in leaving her shelter.

Evelyn read for a few more minutes, then turned off her light and rolled over onto her side. She was sound asleep the moment she shut her eyes.

Despite the noise of the storm, Evelyn slept like a baby, dreaming of electric sheep.

THE NEXT MORNING, EVELYN WOKE UP TO THE SOUND OF chirping birds. The sun shined brightly through her bedroom window. The storm had passed.

Evelyn heard Beulah snoring nearby. At some point in the night, Beulah had left her shelter under the bed and curled up into a ball at Evelyn's feet.

Evelyn climbed out of bed, got dressed, and headed into the kitchen for breakfast. She poured a large bowl of muesli and flipped on the television.

"This was the worst storm to hit our area in almost a hundred years," the news anchor said. "Storm surge and torrential rains have caused the river to overrun its banks, flooding downtown Portsbury."

Evelyn spun her chair around toward the television. "Whoa!" she gasped.

Evelyn's mother entered the room and pulled up a chair to join her.

On the television, images of downtown Portsbury showed Main Street ankle-deep in muddy water.

Next, they showed a news reporter with a microphone standing on the beach, surrounded by mounds of rubble and debris.

"This is Sarah Broche, reporting from Sapphire Beach," the reporter announced. "Last night's storm produced a storm surge, huge waves, and winds up to 85 miles per hour."

"As you can see," the reporter added, waving an arm out toward the ocean, "the beachfront is severely eroded. Many sand dunes have been completely washed away!"

Evelyn began picking all of the raisins out of her bowl of muesli, placing them on her napkin. She always liked to eat the raisins separately.

"Oh, I see you," she said as she used her spoon to dig out a rogue raisin. "Any more of you guys hiding in there?"

Suddenly, Evelyn paused and looked at the television again.

She gasped loudly and then leapt up out of her chair.

"Beulah!" she hollered. "We have a new mission!"

Beulah met her at the door to the garage, where Evelyn

grabbed her backpack and Beulah's leash from hooks on the wall nearby.

"Where are you going?" her mother asked.

"We're off to put my new invention to the ultimate test!" Evelyn announced.

Evelyn collected the Detectorosa 850 and a mini-shovel from the garage.

"Let's go!" Evelyn commanded as she pushed the button to open the garage door.

EVELYN SPED THROUGH HER NEIGHBORHOOD ON HER homemade, electric, off-road skateboard, zooming through deep puddles and making giant splashes. Evelyn carried the Detectorosa 850 in her hands while the mini-shovel was strapped to her backpack.

Beulah ran alongside Evelyn at top speed, her waggly tongue flapping in the wind. Beulah was ecstatic—she loved missions! Even when she didn't know what the mission was!

The two soon arrived at Sapphire Beach. Just like the reporter had said, the beach looked like a disaster zone. Evelyn skidded to a stop and paused to take in the scene. She had never seen anything like it!

Seaweed was scattered across the beach, and a few crab traps had been pushed up onto the shore as well. There were large pieces of driftwood everywhere.

"Oh, my!" cried Evelyn, upon seeing that a dozen boats had been lifted by the storm and dropped down onto land, now a few hundred feet from the edge of the water!

"Perfect!" said Evelyn.

Beulah looked up at her and tilted her head to one side.

"You see," said Evelyn, turning her attention to Beulah, "big storms move stuff around and uncover things, or sometimes bring stuff up onto the beach that's been underwater for years, or even centuries."

"It's the perfect time to go coin shooting," Evelyn continued.

Beulah stared at her.

"Coin shooting means looking for coins with a metal detector."

"And that's why we're here!" she said, smiling broadly, as she proudly held up her new Detectorosa 850.

Evelyn began drawing in the sand with her finger. "First, we'll map out a search pattern."

After finishing her search pattern, Evelyn turned on the Detectorosa 850, and she and Beulah began their search. She carefully walked in straight lines, in order to make sure she didn't miss any places under the sweeping head of her detector.

Within minutes, the Detectorosa 850 emitted a loud "BEEP!" Beulah barked excitedly. Evelyn set down the detector, knelt down, and used her mini-shovel to dig into the sand beneath the spot where the detector had beeped.

"Look! A coin!" Evelyn announced as she brushed off a quarter and then dropped it into a sack she used for any treasures she digs up. "Our first catch of the day!"

EVELYN AND BEULAH CONTINUED SEARCHING UP AND DOWN THE beach, in neat, straight rows, for two hours. They dug up a few coins, a silver ring, a metal button, a key, and a pair of sunglasses.

"Perfect fit!" Evelyn said as she put on the sunglasses. It turned out to be a very sunny day, so she was pleased to have a pair to wear.

They continued to search and dig, and they were having a blast.

The Detectorosa 850 let out a particularly loud "BEEP!" near a chunk of driftwood. Once again, Evelyn began to dig. She kept digging until she saw the edge of a metal object.

"Cool!" she exclaimed as she pulled an old tattered license plate from the sand below. It was a license plate from 1927!

"Now, this is a real treasure," Evelyn beamed as she placed the old license plate into the sack.

"This has been a very fruitful adventure," she said.

Beulah barked in agreement.

"I'm starving!" Evelyn said as she packed up her gear. "Let's go home for lunch."

She removed her new sunglasses to examine the contents of her sack more closely. Just then, a seagull swooped down and snatched the sunglasses from her hand!

Beulah went berserk, barking like mad and chasing after the seagull... no bird was going to get away with stealing from them while Beulah was on duty!

Evelyn hopped onto her skateboard chasing after Beulah and the seagull. The skateboard's chunky off-road tires tore through the sand with ease. With the Detectorosa 850 in one hand and Beulah's leash in the other, Evelyn sped up the beach, laughing hysterically at her silly dog.

Evelyn pointed Detectorosa 850 at the ground as she zoomed along the beach.

"I might as well kill two birds with one stone," she thought. If she was going to cover that much ground, she might as well be scanning for valuables.

Suddenly, the Detectorosa 850 beeped loudly—and multiple times. Even as she sped along, it continued:

BEEEEEEEEEEEEEEEP!

"Whoa!" Evelyn skid to a halt, sending sand flying everywhere. Whatever was buried in the sand nearby had to be very large.

"Beulah!" she yelled into the distance. "Let the seagull go!"

"I've got another pair of shades. There's something huge buried back there," she murmured to herself.

Beulah stopped chasing the seagull and ran back to where Evelyn was waiting for her.

Evelyn and Beulah retraced the path Evelyn had taken on

her skateboard to find the first point where she heard the loud beep.

Once again, they heard a loud "BEEEEEP!"

Evelyn took a few steps and the Detectorosa 850's beeping sound got even louder. She swept the detector head from side to side. Sometimes it would beep, and other times it was silent.

"Strange," said Evelyn, as she tried to determine the edges of the beeping area.

She and Beulah walked in a circular pattern, fanning out a few feet each time. The Detectorosa 850 beeped continuously during some parts, separated by long silences. Whatever metal was in the sand beneath them was massive—but the silent areas suggested it was not one solid piece of metal.

"Maybe there's more than one object," said Evelyn. "There's some sort of pattern here. It almost looks like a big box, or maybe a frame. Either way, it's huge... 50 feet long."

Evelyn stopped searching, knelt down, and took off her backpack. She opened it and fished around, looking for something.

Beulah sat upright, quite certain Evelyn must be searching for the dog's mid-morning doggie treat.

"Here it is!" Evelyn announced. She held up a pad of graph paper and pencil.

Beulah sniffed the pad and pencil, just to make sure it was not a doggie treat. She looked at Evelyn, using her "sad dog" eyes.

"It's true," Evelyn said. "I really do always carry graph paper. You never know when you're going to need it. And, well, here we are, in the middle of a beach after a hurricane, and we need graph paper."

Beulah lay down and sniffed at a bit of seaweed, biting at flies as they flew away.

"First, we'll draw a grid in the sand that corresponds to the graph paper. Then we'll shade in the squares that beep on the Detectorosa 850. That should give us a general idea of the shape of this giant thing, whatever it is."

After Evelyn finished drawing a grid in the sand using a stick, she turned on the Detectorosa 850 and began walking, row by row, over the grid.

Each time the Detectorosa 850 beeped loudly, she stopped and shaded the area on her graph paper.

Row by row she went, filling in some squares on her graph paper, while leaving others blank. Slowly, an image began to appear.

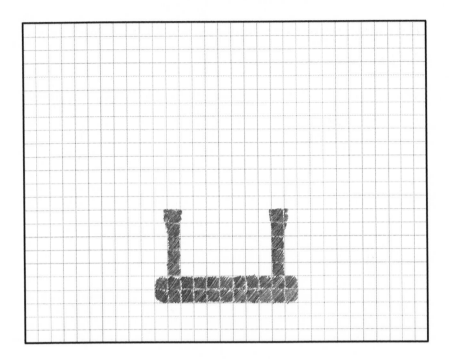

Evelyn stopped suddenly. She held up the picture and studied it carefully.

"Could it be?" Evelyn gasped, as she looked down at the shaded graph paper. Evelyn quickly leapt up and started sweeping the area with Detectorosa 850.

But this time, instead of using her systematic grid search pattern, she had a better idea of where to look, and she traced out the entire object's outline, filling in her graph paper as she went.

And suddenly, there it was. Evelyn stopped scanning the ground and stared in bewilderment at the completed shape that filled her graph paper drawing.

"No way. It's simply not possible!"

"Beulah! Let's start digging, right over here, in this spot," Evelyn said, as she grabbed her shovel and began digging in one of the sections that was shaded on the graph paper.

Beulah barked excitedly and began to dig alongside her.

The two kept digging for several minutes. Suddenly, Evelyn's shovel hit something made of metal.

CLUNK!!

Evelyn and Beulah stopped digging and looked at each other. Evelyn reached down and touched a metal object. She knew exactly what it was.

"I don't believe it!" Evelyn cried out. "This can't be happening!" Evelyn was so happy, she fought to hold back tears of joy.

She quickly pushed the sand back into the hole they had dug. Beulah was confused.

"Sorry, pup," Evelyn said to Beulah. "This is way too big for you and me. We're going to need some help."

Evelyn looked around, suddenly mindful of who might have seen them digging. There were plenty of people up on the land, assessing storm damage, but few people were on the beach, and none were in this deserted area where the seagull had led them.

Beulah paused and watched Evelyn, unsure of what she had in mind.

Evelyn reached for her phone and sent a top-secret, coded message to her best friends, the girls of STEAMTeam 5: Sandia Scientist, Treeka Technologist, Ariana Artist, and Mattie Mathematician.

The message read:

CODE RED: I FOUND A BURIED TREASURE!

5

CODE RED

*E*velyn hooked the leash to Beulah's collar and jumped onto her skateboard. Within seconds, they were flying down the beach, back toward Evelyn's house.

EVELYN RAN INTO HER HOUSE, PANTING FROM A COMBINATION of exhaustion and excitement.

"Mom!" Evelyn shouted after closing the front door.

Her mother quickly appeared in the entryway. She was wearing her earpiece. Evelyn winced. She didn't know she was on a phone call.

"Oops!" she whispered. She mouthed a "Sorry."

"I'm on mute,'" her mother assured her. "Everything okay?"

"I'll explain when you're done," Evelyn replied in a whisper as she hurried to her bedroom.

"The girls arrived 10 minutes ago," her mom said. "They're waiting in your room."

"Excellent!" Evelyn beamed as she rushed down the hallway toward her bedroom, grabbing a doggie treat from a jar along the way. She tossed it to Beulah, who caught the treat in mid-air without missing a beat, as she ran alongside Evelyn.

When Evelyn entered her room, there were four eager faces smiling at her. Her friends—Sandia, Treeka, Ariana, and Mattie were lounging around, chatting.

Suddenly, they all went quiet.

Evelyn grinned. She was excited to tell her best friends about her incredible discovery on the beach.

"We got your emergency message... dish!" said Mattie. The others nodded eagerly.

"As you know," Evelyn began, "last night was one of the worst storms to ever hit this part of the country."

"They said it's one for the history books!" Sandia exclaimed.

"That's right," said Evelyn. "And when big storms hit the

beach, they can move tons of sand. Sometimes even alter the coastline!"

"I knew it... you've found Atlantis!" Treeka cut in.

"A pirate ship!" shouted Mattie.

"A crashed alien spacecraft!" Sandia cried, full of hope.

Everyone looked at Ariana. She had not yet offered a guess.

"Um... A wooden chest full of gold coins and jewels and stuff?" said Ariana, meekly.

"That's it!" said Treeka. "Treasure! Ariana is saying 'treasure.'"

Evelyn pulled the graph paper from her backpack and placed it upside-down on the desk next to her. Nobody could see what was drawn on the down-facing side. She smiled broadly.

"Yesterday, I built a metal detector out of a weed whacker."

"A weed what?" asked Treeka.

"Whacker," Evelyn replied. "It's a thing you do yardwork with. Not important. What is important is that, this morning, I was digging up raisins in my cereal and I realized, 'Hey, we had a big storm, and I'll bet today would be a good day to hunt for coins down at the beach.'"

"And you found Atlantis!" said Treeka.

"Atlantis was probably the Greek island of Santorini," said Sandia. "It was destroyed by a volcano, the Minoan Eruption, around 1500 BCE."

"That," Evelyn resumed, "... and my top-secret coded message said I found a buried treasure, not a lost civilization."

"All good points," Treeka conceded. "I'm changing my vote to treasure. Ariana and I say treasure! The gold and jewels kind!"

"Pirate treasure!" said Mattie, slightly modifying her guess from pirate ship.

"So, you found some kind of treasure... on the beach?" Sandia asked.

"A treasure of sorts, yes!" said Evelyn. "Something huge, buried in the sand!" she continued, tapping on the piece of graph paper.

"Show. Us. The. Graph. Paper!" pleaded Ariana. She felt as though she was going to burst if she had to wait another minute. The other girls nodded excitedly.

"Well," said Evelyn, "at first, I wasn't sure what I had found. It was BIG... fifty feet across! But its shape seemed really weird. So I drew a giant grid on the sand and then filled in a square on this graph paper wherever my metal detector beeped."

Evelyn slowly turned over the paper for the girls to see.

"And here's what I found, buried in the sand..."

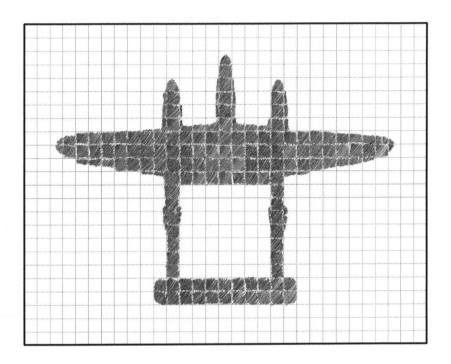

"Whooooaa!" said the girls, in unison.

"An airplane!" said Mattie. "How on earth did that get there?"

"Not just any plane," Evelyn gushed. *"It's a P-38 Lightning!"*

The girls just sat there with blank expressions.

"One sec!" Evelyn spun around and grabbed a large, heavy book from her bookshelf. The book's title was "Warbirds."

She placed the book on her bed with a loud *THUMP* and flipped it open to page 117.

The others watched intently.

"See this outline? It's a P-38 Lightning!" Evelyn exclaimed, as she held the book up for her friends to see.

Evelyn placed the graph paper next to a diagram on page 117. The shaded areas formed the exact same shape as the plane in the diagram!

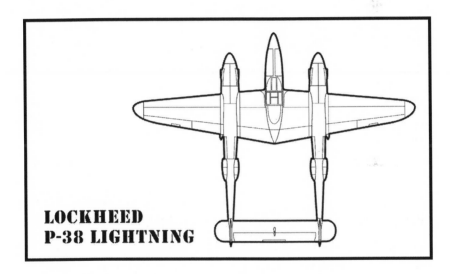

LOCKHEED
P-38 LIGHTNING

"It's an exact match!" said Ariana.

"Bingo!" Evelyn announced. "See the twin booms? And the center section where the pilot sits? It's a very distinctive design."

"At first, I thought there might be two planes, or maybe one plane that broke into two pieces. But when I filled in all the squares, I saw the complete picture. I knew it could only be a P-38!"

The girls huddled around the book to compare the image on the graph paper with the one in the book.

"The Lockheed P-38 Lightning," said Evelyn. "It's a very famous World War II fighter plane."

"What made it so special?" asked Mattie.

"The P-38 was one of the most feared fighter escorts during World War II," Evelyn explained.

"Its twin-boom design was very unusual," she continued. "Having two engines meant it could fly higher and faster than other fighters. With extra fuel tanks under the wings, it could fly really far, too."

"They even recorded a P-38 engine for the sound of the speeder bikes in Return of the Jedi," said Evelyn.

"Whoa, " Treeka said. "On Endor?"

"The Forest Moon of," said Evelyn, nodding.

"They built ten thousand P-38s in World War II," she concluded.

"Wow," said Mattie. "That's a whole lot of airplanes! What happened to all of them?"

"They're mostly all gone," said Evelyn, a hint of sadness in her voice. "There are only a couple dozen that still exist today."

"And you found one!" exclaimed Ariana.

Evelyn looked a little dazed. Her giant discovery was still setting in.

"Right there in the sand, for all these years. I can't believe the plane even exists!" said Evelyn. "Let alone that I found it... with... a homemade metal detector."

"That you made out of a weed smacker," said Treeka.

"Weed wacker," said Evelyn.

"How far down do you think the airplane is buried?" asked Sandia.

"Not deep at all," Evelyn replied, "I dug down in the sand a couple of feet and reached the top of a tail fin, right where you'd expect it to be." Evelyn pointed at a spot on the P-38 diagram in the book.

"And then, I filled the hole back up, and came to tell you guys. I have no idea what to do next."

Sandia slid into a chair next to Evelyn.

"Tell us more about how you found this plane," she asked.

"Well, I was down at the beach—looking for coins with a metal detector," explained Evelyn. "I found a bunch of cool stuff, like this old license plate." She reached into her backpack and pulled out the license plate for the others to see.

"Whoa, cool!" beamed Treeka. "*1927!*"

Mattie looked closely at the old license plate. "You found this with a metal detector?" she asked.

"Not just a metal detector, my new Detectorosa 850!" said Evelyn, proudly holding up her latest invention for all to see.

"Nice!" said Treeka.

Evelyn handed the metal detector to Treeka so she could take a closer look.

Treeka turned on the Detectorosa 850 and began scanning the room. She waved it over a metal lamp. The detector beeped loudly. The girls all let out squeals of joy.

"This is awesome," said Treeka, nodding her head with approval. "I'm gonna need one."

"As I mentioned," Evelyn continued, "after a big storm, sometimes you can find cool stuff. Stuff that either gets washed up on the beach, or uncovered because sand gets washed away."

"I had just built the Detectorosa 850 to find my wrench that Beulah buried..."

"Beulah buried a wrench?" Mattie asked.

"It's a long story," Evelyn replied.

They all nodded knowingly. Everyone with pets knows that furry babies can be quite mischievous.

"Anyway," Evelyn continued, "I thought 'Hey, I have a metal detector. I should go down to the beach and do some treasure hunting.'"

The other four girls nodded vigorously in agreement.

"So, I searched the beach for a couple hours and then rode way up the beach on my skateboard when Beulah chased a seagull. Suddenly, Detectorosa 850 started beeping like crazy. The signal was so loud, and covered such a large area, I knew it had to be something really big," Evelyn explained.

By now, all of the girls were facing Evelyn and hanging on her every word.

"That's when I drew a grid and scanned every square, leading to the picture."

"So, do you think this plane washed up on the beach during last night's storm?" Sandia asked.

"No," Evelyn replied. "I think it's been buried there for a long time."

"But here's the million-dollar question," she continued. "How does a World War II-era fighter plane end up buried on our beach, for over seventy years, and nobody knows about it?"

The girls all pondered this. It was quite a puzzle, indeed.

"I've been giving this a lot of thought," Evelyn said. "And I think I know the answer."

6

THE HYPOTHESIS

"There are a few possibilities to choose from," Evelyn began.

"First, the plane might have been landed or crashed on the beach and later covered by sand. The plane's shape I drew looks pretty intact, so I don't think it crashed, at least not badly. If we dig the plane up..."

"You mean *when* we dig the plane up!" Treeka interjected.

"*When* we dig the plane up," Evelyn said with a smile, "we'll learn more about the plane's condition, and whether the landing gear is up or down. A landing gear in the down position and unbroken would mean the plane landed normally."

The girls all nodded. Evelyn continued.

"But I'm guessing the plane didn't land or crash on the beach. If it had crashed, people would have known about it. And if it had landed safely, I'm pretty sure the military would have come and gotten their plane."

"So if it didn't land on the beach," Mattie asked, "where did it land?"

Evelyn nodded. "The other option is that it could have landed—or crashed—in shallow water, and sank, and then been moved over time by currents, shifting sand, and other geological forces.

"The coastline might have changed in seventy years. Something a hundred yards out to sea, back then, might be located where the beach is today. That's what I think happened. "

"Can P-38s land in water?" Sandia asked.

"Sort of," replied Evelyn. "It's called a 'belly landing,' which is really more like a controlled crash. It means the pilot sets the plane down gently—on the water, in this case. He lands with the landing gear up, so the plane is smooth on the bottom. The plane might never fly again, but it's better than crashing straight into the water at high speed."

"Would the pilot survive?" asked Ariana.

"Probably not if it crashed hard," said Evelyn. "But, if he belly landed on the water, there's a good chance he could have gotten out before it sank. And then swam to shore, if it wasn't too far."

"Why didn't you dig up the plane?" Treeka asked.

"Oh, it's way too big," said Evelyn. "Besides, I was afraid to damage it. This is a job for professional archaeologists. It belongs in a museum or something."

"And... it's possible that the pilot..." Evelyn trailed off, unsure how to say what she was thinking.

"Never made it home?" Sandia asked.

"Yes," said Evelyn. She loved how Sandia always managed to be so sweet, even when she had something difficult to say.

They all sat in silence for a while.

Treeka flipped the page of Evelyn's Warbirds book and looked at more photographs of P-38s.

"We should tell someone—you know, in case there's a war hero in there or something," Treeka suggested.

"I agree," said Evelyn. The others all nodded. "But remember, whoever flew this plane might have survived!"

"Really?" Sandia asked, her voice full of hope. "Do you really think so?"

"Sure!" Evelyn answered. "Have you guys ever heard about Glacier Girl?"

"Who?" Mattie asked.

"She sounds cold," Ariana added, with a giggle.

"Glacier Girl and her pilot survived a crash in a P-38 in 1942 —in fact, six P-38s made an emergency landing on the ice in Greenland. They called them the Lost Squadron," Evelyn began.

The others watched Evelyn intently as she continued.

"The crew were all rescued, thank goodness," Evelyn added. "But they had to leave the planes right there, on the ice. And over the next forty years, the planes gradually got covered under 260 feet of ice."

Treeka mouthed the word "Wow."

Evelyn continued. "Back in the 1980's, aviation enthusiasts located one of the planes, called Glacier Girl. They dug a hole in the ice and brought her up to the surface!"

"Whoa!" said the girls.

"Two feet of sand suddenly doesn't sound too bad," chuckled Treeka.

"And get this..." Evelyn said excitedly. "They fully restored Glacier Girl, and she still flies to this day!"

"That's insane!" Ariana blurted. "I think we should find out more about our plane that's been hidden under the sand for seventy years. It's got to have quite a story behind it!"

Sandia nodded her head in agreement. "Well, we already know it's a P-38, thanks to Evelyn's encyclopedic knowledge of airplane shapes."

Evelyn smiled at the compliment.

"Now we know *what* it is," said Sandia. "But we don't know who it belonged to, or why it's there."

"I say we find out!" Mattie insisted.

"I'm in!" Treeka added.

"Me too!" blurted Ariana.

"I already have a hypothesis to test," Evelyn said.

"So, what's your hypothesis?" ask Sandia. As the scientist of the group, she always recommended coming up with a hypothesis as the first step to solving any problem or mystery.

"My hypothesis," started Evelyn, "is that the pilot was headed to Flint Falls, but he didn't make it. Maybe a mechanical failure, or maybe he ran out of fuel."

"Maybe he got shot down!" said Treeka.

"Not likely," said Evelyn. "I don't think there were any battles this close to the mainland."

"Where did you say he might have been headed?" Ariana asked.

"Flint Falls Airfield," replied Evelyn. "It's a tiny airstrip, about six miles from here."

"That airport's been around that long?" Mattie asked.

"Longer actually, since 1928," Evelyn answered. "It was used a lot during the war, patrolling the coast for enemy submarines."

"Hey, didn't your great-grandmother work there?" Ariana asked Evelyn.

"She sure did," Evelyn answered.

"Let's call Grandma Helen!" commanded Sandia.

"That's just what I was thinking!" replied Evelyn, picking up her phone.

Evelyn clicked a single button on her phone to speed-dial her great-grandmother.

"Grandma, you're not going to believe what I found at the beach today!"

7

THE GREATEST GENERATION

"Grandma Helen should be here in about an hour," Evelyn told the others, as she slipped her phone into her front pocket. "She's so excited about helping us with this."

"While we're waiting," began Mattie, "what else did you find with your metal detector?"

Evelyn retrieved her collection bag from her backpack and poured out all of the treasures she had collected from the beach into an empty shoe box. The objects included a silver ring, an old key, coins, buttons, and an assortment of little metal parts.

Ariana, the group's photographer, snapped a photo of the items.

The girls were utterly fascinated... it was like looking back through time. They examined each item with great care, one by one, inventing possible stories about each of the lost treasures and their mysterious, former owners.

Sandia invented a whole story around the silver ring, about a young man who proposed to his sweetheart, long ago, on the beach...

"And then a killer whale got them!" cried Treeka, and the girls all laughed hysterically.

Just then, Evelyn's mother knocked on the bedroom door, then opened it.

"Look who's here..." she said, as she held the door open for Grandma Helen.

"Grandma!" Evelyn rejoiced, leaping up to give her a giant hug. It had only been a day since she'd seen her great-grandmother, but she was always so happy to see her.

"Hi girls!" Grandma Helen beamed. "I'm here for an adventure!" she grinned.

All of the girls began talking at once.

"Evelyn found an airplane!" Treeka bellowed.

"And a bunch of money!" Mattie added.

"And a silver ring!" said Sandia.

"That's all so great to hear!" Grandma Helen replied.

The girls reshuffled themselves on the bed to make room for Grandma Helen to sit.

"How can I help?" Grandma Helen asked. "Evelyn, you hinted something about an airplane on the phone... you were quite mysterious. I must admit, you've piqued my curiosity."

Evelyn repeated the story that she had told her friends, about how she found a massive object on the beach using her metal detector.

Then, Evelyn slowly reached for the graph paper sketch, and held it up so her great-grandmother could see it.

Grandma Helen put on her glasses and took the paper in her hand, then suddenly let out a gasp.

"Oh my, good heavens... this is a P-38! You've found a Lightning, my dear Evelyn!" she cried.

The girls were impressed. Grandma Helen knew her stuff.

"Evelyn has a hypothesis," Sandia said, "that the pilot was headed for a nearby airfield, but didn't make it.

"I see," Grandma Helen. "Which airfield?"

"Flint Falls," said Evelyn. "And that's why we called you."

"Remarkable," said Grandma Helen.

The old woman took one last look at the graph paper drawing of the P-38 and then removed her glasses. She looked up at all of the girls.

"We used to see quite a few P-38s at Flint Falls, back in the day."

"See?!" Evelyn blurted.

Grandma Helen laughed. "Well, we weren't the only airstrip on the west coast. But it's a good hypothesis. How do you plan to test it?"

"Well," said Evelyn, "I was hoping you could help us since you used to work there."

"Yes, I sure did. Worked there in the late 40's—after the war," Grandma Helen replied.

"What did you do there?" asked Mattie.

"Were you in the Air Force?" Treeka asked.

"At that time—in 1947—the Air Force didn't accept women," Grandma Helen explained.

"Boo!" Treeka replied.

"Yes, boo!" Grandma Helen repeated with a smile. "I was in the Army—the Women's Army Corps," Grandma Helen explained. "We served in the Army but performed Air Force duties."

"Did you fly planes?" asked Ariana.

"No," Grandma Helen replied. "Those were the WAFs—that program came along a bit later, in 1948."

"Then what did you do?" Mattie asked.

"I was a mechanic!" Grandma Helen answered proudly.

A broad smile spread across Evelyn's face. "It runs in the family."

"It certainly does," Grandma Helen replied.

"My daughter, Margot—Evelyn's grandmother, was an electrical engineer. She worked for an electric company for 35 years," Grandma Helen told the others.

"And my mother is an engineer, too!" Evelyn exclaimed.

"And, of course, Evelyn, is our latest engineer—and inventor!" Grandma Helen replied, joyfully.

Evelyn smiled.

"That's so great!" said Sandia.

The others nodded in agreement. It was pretty neat to have four generations of women engineers in the family.

Grandma Helen clapped her hands together. "So, how can this old engineer help you? I'm not much of a digger these days," she said with a chuckle.

Evelyn laughed. "I was hoping you might know someone who knows something about the planes that used to land at Flint Falls. You know, maybe someone who could check the records about missing planes or tell us who it might belong to."

"Hmmm," Grandma Helen said, as she closed her eyes to concentrate. "It was so long ago. Unfortunately, I don't think there are many people still alive who would know."

Grandma Helen's eyes twinkled with a hint of sadness.

"Oh, I hope I didn't make you sad to think about it, Grandma," Evelyn said, placing her arm around her.

"It's bittersweet—so many good memories," Grandma Helen replied. "But it's okay, I promise," she added with a soft smile.

Suddenly, Grandma Helen snapped her fingers and pointed into the air. "Of course! George!"

Evelyn tilted her head in curiosity.

"George Lee—I believe he was involved with a Warbird

Recovery and Restoration project!" Grandma Helen proclaimed.

"George Lee?" Evelyn asked.

"He's in my Mahjong club," said Grandma Helen. "Surely, he could help!"

"I tell you what, let's head over to the Community Center and talk to him. He loves company," Grandma Helen suggested.

"I'll ask mom to drive us!" said Evelyn as she raced out of the room.

THE SUN WAS JUST BEGINNING TO SET WHEN THEY ALL ARRIVED at Sage Village, Grandma Helen's retirement home.

The girls hopped out of Evelyn's mother's burgundy SUV and raced toward the entrance. Evelyn's mother helped Grandma Helen out of the car.

"Have fun, everybody," said Evelyn's mom. "I'll be back to pick you up in two hours."

They all waved goodbye as Evelyn's mom drove away.

Grandma Helen was as sprite as someone half her age, and she made sure that everyone knew it. Although she used a cane, she explained that it was "only a backup."

Grandma Helen shuffled quickly along the path, waving at her fellow residents as they passed by.

All of Grandma's friends greeted the girls the moment they entered the building.

"Look how big you are!" exclaimed one of Grandma Helen's friends when she saw Evelyn. "You're almost all grown up!"

Evelyn smiled. She enjoyed visiting the place. Everyone was always so happy to see her.

"Has anyone seen George?" Grandma Helen asked the group of people who had gathered around them.

A woman answered. "He's in the main hall, helping them set up for the concert tonight."

"Follow me," Grandma Helen instructed the girls.

Evelyn and her friends trailed behind Grandma Helen as she walked slowly but confidently down a long hallway. They could hear music coming from the large room up ahead.

"George is good with electronics," Grandma Helen commented as they walked. "Almost as good as me," she added with a wink.

As they approached the large room, Grandma Helen knocked on the open door with her cane. A man in his late seventies spun around in surprise.

"Helen!" cheered George. "And you brought the kids!"

George waved them all into the room.

"What a nice surprise," said George.

"We're on a mission," said Grandma Helen.

"A mission, huh?" George said. This got his attention. He had known Grandma Helen for ten years, and she was, by far, the most adventurous resident at Sage Village.

"And we want you to join us," Grandma Helen answered.

"Whatever it is, you can count me in," said George. "Let's go grab some coffee."

A few minutes later, they were all seated around a circular table in the deserted coffee lounge.

"No one will overhear us in here," Grandma Helen said to George. "We're trying to keep this hush-hush for now."

George understood. He nodded in agreement. "So, what IS this secret mission?" he asked, leaning in eagerly.

"Why don't you explain, Evelyn," Grandma Helen replied.

Evelyn cleared her throat. "The storm last night was so powerful that it moved a bunch of..."

Evelyn stopped and glanced over at Sandia before correcting

herself. *"It's our hypothesis* that the storm moved a bunch of sand and almost revealed the wreckage of an old airplane."

"Oh my!" George gasped. He looked at Grandma Helen without saying another word.

Evelyn continued. "I used my new metal detector..."

"Which she made," Grandma Helen interjected, smiling with pride.

"Yes, which I made," Evelyn repeated. "I was coin hunting on the beach, and I discovered a large object... very large."

George nodded his head, eager to hear more.

"I mapped out the shape of the object," she said. Evelyn carefully removed her graph paper drawing from her backpack and handed it to George.

"By Jove! That's fantastic!" George bellowed. "Impossible! Do you know what this is?"

"A P-38" said Grandma Helen, Evelyn, and the other girls, in unison.

George just stared at the drawing, squinting to detect the slightest details, even though it was a very rough sketch.

At last, he spoke.

"You found this right here? On our very own Sapphire Beach?"

Evelyn nodded.

"But we're not sure what to do now," Evelyn explained. "Grandma Helen said you're an expert on this sort of thing."

George sat back in this chair, thinking. He took a sip of his coffee. After several seconds, he leaned forward again. There was an eagerness in his eyes and the slightest trace of a smile.

"We're gonna dig it up!" he whispered.

8

CONFIRMATION

"Do you have equipment to dig up a plane?" Sandia asked.

"Well, no," George replied. "But I know people who do."

"I told these girls you've been involved with recovering old aircraft," said Grandma Helen.

"Yes, indeed," said George. "It's been a few years, but I do know a bit about warbird recovery."

"And restoration?!" Ariana asked.

"That too," George replied. "But, first things first—we need to protect the site. Evelyn, have you told anyone else about your discovery?"

"No," said Evelyn.

"That's good," George replied. "I'll talk to Paula Youngblood. She's an archaeologist with the Historic Preservation Commission. And my friend, Davis James. I worked with him on a warbird recovery project many years ago in the Solomon Islands. He's a leader in this field."

"Welcome to the team!" Evelyn announced, extending her hand to George. He took her hand in his and shook it vigorously, grinning ear to ear.

George stood up suddenly. "Now, if you'll excuse me, I've got to go start making some phone calls. Should only take an hour or so, if you'd like to wait."

"Perfect," said Grandma Helen. "I'm starved, and I'll bet these girls are, too. We'll be in my apartment eating strawberry ice cream."

ALMOST EXACTLY AN HOUR LATER, GEORGE KNOCKED LIGHTLY on the door to Grandma Helen's apartment. The girls were just finishing their second bowls of ice cream.

"It's George!" Grandma Helen announced as she opened the door.

George stepped into the apartment and shut the door behind him. His face had no expression whatsoever. Everyone looked at him, anxious to hear the results of his phone calls.

Suddenly, George made a big "thumbs up" symbol and smiled broadly.

"It's a go!" he said, delighted.

Grandma Helen and the girls were elated to hear this.

"Paula Youngblood will get the permits, which should only take a few days. Davis James said he can drive up from San Francisco by then. His organization has volunteers and can fund the excavation. *That is, if...*" George paused.

"If it is... what we think it is," he finished.

"You mean, a P-38?" Evelyn asked.

"Yes," said George. "We'll need to take a look at the site before we set all this in motion."

"You bet!" said Evelyn. "Want to go right now? I'm positive I can find it again in the dark!"

George laughed and said, "Ha, no, that's okay. It's getting a little late. But how about, say, 6 o'clock tomorrow morning? Meet at the Sapphire Beach parking lot?"

Evelyn looked at Grandma Helen and the others. They all

nodded excitedly, with big smiles. Evelyn looked back at George.

"Six a.m., Sapphire Beach," she said. "We'll be there!"

THE NEXT MORNING, EVELYN'S MOM'S BURGUNDY SUV WAS fully loaded with Grandma Helen and the members of STEAMTeam 5, all quietly enjoying cocoa and warm blueberry muffins, as they made their way to Sapphire Beach.

No one spoke a word for the first few minutes. They were all still trying to wake up. Except for Treeka, who was sound asleep.

"Right around the bend here," Evelyn said to her mother, who was driving them.

They pulled into the parking lot at Sapphire Beach at precisely 5:57a.m. The beach was deserted, except for a couple of surfers sitting on their boards, waiting for a wave.

The small parking lot was empty except for one car. George Lee was already there, standing next to it. He wore a baseball cap and sunglasses. A woman stood next to him.

George waved at the girls as they climbed out of Evelyn's mom's SUV.

George introduced everyone, saving Evelyn for last.

"Paula Youngblood," this is my friend Helen and her great-granddaughter, Evelyn. Evelyn is the engineer I told you about!" George announced.

Paula Youngblood was in her early fifties. She had black, shoulder-length hair and deep brown eyes.

"Nice to meet you, Evelyn! I'm Paula!"

Evelyn said hello and shook Paula's hand.

"I hear you might have found an airplane!" Paula said to Evelyn.

"Not just any airplane," said Evelyn, with a smile.

"Let's go take a look!" said George. "I can hardly wait!"

Evelyn reached into the back seat of the SUV. She reappeared with the Detectorosa 850 in one hand and her mini-shovel in the other.

The group walked up the beach for about fifteen minutes until they reached the place where Evelyn had drawn her grid in the sand the day before. It appeared to be undisturbed.

"It looks just like it did when I left it," said Evelyn.

George pointed to a line of seaweed between the grid and the ocean.

"See that down there? That's the high tide mark from last night," he said. He pulled a small booklet out of his back pocket and flipped through it until he came to the right page.

"Looks like we're in luck," he said. "Your airplane is well above high tide, Evelyn."

Evelyn smiled. She liked how George had called it "her" airplane.

"There might be water when we dig down far enough," George continued, "but at least we won't be fighting the tide every day up here on the surface. That means the excavation will go much faster, and cost less money."

"Evelyn," George continued, "would you like to show me how you made your grid drawing of the plane with your metal detector?"

"Absolutely!" said Evelyn.

She took her graph paper drawing out of her pocket, unfolded it, and handed it to George. She then proceeded to walk up and down the grid pattern in the sand. As the Detectorosa 850 alternated between beeps and silence, George traced his finger along the corresponding square on the paper.

"Your drawing is very accurate!" George said to Evelyn.

She smiled as the two continued walking the grid. The others stood off to the side and watched.

When George and Evelyn finished the entire grid, they walked back to the others, who were waiting eagerly.

"What's the verdict, George?" Paula asked.

"Well," replied George, "either somebody has created an elaborate hoax by burying a bunch of metal in the exact shape of a P-38 Lightning..."

George paused for effect.

"Or... Evelyn has found herself... *AN ACTUAL, P-38 LIGHT-NING, right here on Sapphire Beach!*" he cried out loud. He then shouted at the top of his lungs, "*Yeeee-haaaaw,*" and started hooting and hollering and dancing around, giving everybody hugs and high-fives.

The girls all screamed in excitement, jumping up and down, barely able to contain themselves. Even Grandma Helen got in on the action, and did a little jig. With her cane, of course. (But only as a backup.)

When the commotion finally died down a bit, Evelyn got George's attention.

"Would you like to see where I dug down and touched the top of the tail fin?" she asked him.

George's eyes opened wide. "You bet I would!" he said.

"Over here," Evelyn said, leading the others to the spot on the grid where she had dug the hole the day before.

"I chose to dig at this spot because the top of the tail fin should be the highest point, if the plane is sitting level."

"Smart girl," said George.

"It's genetic," said Grandma Helen.

Evelyn began to dig using her shovel, just as she had done with Beulah the day before. Sure enough, she soon reached something metal. She backed away so that George could reach down into the hole and feel it for himself.

As George reached down and touched the object, he started to dig a bit more sand out of the hole with his hand, to see more of the metal. He suddenly stopped. His lip trembled just a bit. The girls saw that he was crying.

Paula put her hand on George's shoulder.

"We're going to take good care of her," Paula said to George, referring to the airplane. "Who should we call next?"

George looked at Paula.

"Everybody," he said.

THE NEXT FEW DAYS FELT LIKE TEN YEARS FOR THE GIRLS OF

STEAMTeam 5. While the grownups were busy coordinating a large-scale excavation project, Evelyn and the others had nothing to do but wait.

They dared not visit the airplane's location on the beach, for fear of drawing attention. Before they had left, they once again filled the hole at the top of the tail fin. George had even instructed everybody to kick sand around and erase the grid that marked the plane's location. To anybody who happened to be walking a dog on that lonely stretch of the beach, the location of the plane would look just like any other patch of sand.

To pass the time, the girls read everything they could get their hands on about P-38 Lightnings. Who knew that an airplane could be so exciting! They read stories of bravery, heroism, and tragedy. They even learned that, during the war, over a thousand women were trained as pilots, to deliver (or "ferry") airplanes wherever they needed to go. These women flew lots of P-38s!

Ariana had taken to drawing all kinds of pictures of P-38s, using photos on the Internet and in Evelyn's books for reference. She had never realized that a machine could be so beautiful. And in her own way, she came to feel a connection to the engineers who had designed the plane.

"Mechanical things don't end up beautiful by accident," she

told the others. "They knew what they were doing when they designed her."

And this made Evelyn smile.

AT LAST, THE WAITING WAS OVER. IN THE MORNING, THE GIRLS would return to Sapphire Beach and participate in the excavation of the P-38.

9

THE EXCAVATION

The big day finally arrived. Evelyn and the others would finally get to watch as the P-38 was carefully dug up from the sand, where it had lain, hidden, for seventy years!

Again, the burgundy SUV pulled into the small parking lot.

But this time, the parking lot was full of cars, including a large flatbed truck with a small bulldozer chained onto it.

A group of about twenty people stood around, sipping steaming hot coffee. Evelyn saw George and Paula, but she did not recognize the others. The girls and Grandma Helen got out of the SUV.

"Morning, everyone!" George exclaimed.

"Morning, George!" Grandma Helen replied.

"It's a great day to dig up a plane!" George called out, eliciting a few whistles and some clapping from the crowd.

"Not just any plane," said Paula, giving a sly wink to Evelyn. Evelyn smiled and winked back.

"Every day's a good day to recover a P-38," said a tall, gray-haired man with a beard. He stepped forward out of the crowd and approached the girls.

"Which one of you is Evelyn?" the man asked.

Evelyn stepped forward, holding her Detectorosa 850 and mini-shovel. "I am," she said.

"It's an honor to meet you," said the man, shaking Evelyn's hand. "My name is Davis James. I recover warbirds. My friend George here tells me that you've found one."

He looked down at the objects Evelyn was holding.

"I see you've brought a shovel," said Davis.

Evelyn looked over at the bulldozer chained to the flatbed truck and said with a smile, "I see you've brought one too."

FOUR HOURS LATER, THE SITE OF THE P-38 LOOKED completely different.

The area had been cordoned off with yellow tape to prevent any unauthorized people from getting too close. As official members of the team, the girls of STEAMTeam 5 were given badges and were permitted within the excavation area. Mattie, Treeka, and Sandia were in charge of keeping onlookers—and dogs—from crossing the yellow tape.

With Evelyn's guidance, and her graph paper sketch, a team of archaeologists had recreated her grid pattern in the sand, but this time, using wooden stakes and string. Ariana was the team's official photographer. She snapped photos at every step.

The flatbed truck had driven all the way up the beach to the site, where men unloaded the bulldozer.

But before the bulldozer started moving any sand, the team had dug a bunch of small test holes to confirm that there were no parts of the airplane at risk of being damaged.

Only then did the bulldozer go to work. And over a couple of hours, it removed several tons of sand off of the top of the P-38. But then the bulldozing stopped, long before the pit looked much like anything resembling an airplane. This was to avoid damaging the plane. The excavators then dug many more small holes with shovels to determine the depth of the aircraft at various locations.

And whenever one of these holes actually came into contact with part of the airplane, the digging with shovels stopped and a small team of archaeologists would swoop in and dig very slowly and carefully with little hand shovels.

And when they dug away as much sand as they could without actually touching the airplane, they switched to stiff-bristled brushes and they gently brushed away the sand.

The process was very careful, but painstakingly slow.

THE GIRLS HAD NOT REALIZED HOW MUCH TIME EXCAVATING the P-38 would take. Thankfully, Evelyn's mother had brought beach chairs, umbrellas for shade, and a cooler full of sandwiches, snacks, and lots of bottled water.

The P-38's two tail fins were now exposed, sticking right out of the sand like a pair of round shark fins.

"The tail fins are the highest part of the airplane," Evelyn said to the girls. "They should reach the canopy soon."

"What's a canopy?" asked Treeka.

"It's the windshield, on top of the cockpit, where the pilot sits," said Evelyn.

Sandia suddenly gasped!

"I almost forgot!" she said.

"Forgot what?" asked the others.

"Do you think we'll find..." Sandia stopped, mid-sentence.

"The pilot?" Evelyn asked Sandia.

Sandia nodded.

"Hard to say," said Evelyn. "Not if he made it out safely, of course. And if he didn't, it's hard to know what might still exist after being under water and sand for almost a century."

"Scientists have found well-preserved bones in mountain caves that are thousands of years old!" Sandia added, cheerfully. "But the dry air helped preserve them. Things don't last long in the ocean, unless they happen to become fossilized."

"If the pilot didn't make it out," said Evelyn, "we might be able to know for sure. Even if his body no longer exists, there may be metal objects, such as his I.D. tags, buttons, zippers, maybe a wristwatch, or his sidearm."

This fascinated the girls. They watched the digging crew intently, waiting for them to reach the airplane's canopy.

People walking on the beach occasionally stopped to watch or ask questions.

A jogger passed by with her dog, a large golden retriever. The human stopped running to check out the taped-off area, while the dog sniffed around, doing a bit of digging of her own.

"What's going on?" the jogger asked.

"It's an archaeological site," Sandia explained, using her best "scientist" voice.

"Awesome!" the jogger said as she took a water break.

"What are they looking for?" she asked.

"A plane crashed here 70 years ago," Evelyn answered.

"Wow!" the jogger replied. "Can I see it?"

"Not yet," Evelyn sighed.

"They said it will take several days," Ariana added.

"Many archaeological sites take months, or years, to excavate," Sandia explained. "This one is really quick by comparison."

"I see," the woman replied. "We run here every day, so hopefully we'll get to see it. Good luck with everything!" she said as she trotted away. "Come on, Gracie!"

The golden retriever stopped digging and raced off to catch up with her.

"BINGO!" YELLED ONE OF THE CREW MEMBERS.

It was early afternoon. At last, they had reached the airplane's canopy.

The girls all stood up to get a better look. Soon, they would know whether or not the pilot made it out of the plane.

The archaeologists carefully dug scoops of sand out of the cockpit and sifted the sand in a wooden box with a screen on the bottom. This way, they were sure not to miss any tiny objects.

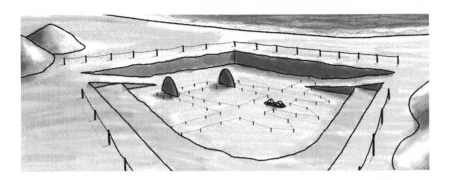

After an hour, they had dug out most of the cockpit. Their sifting box yielded many pebbles and shells... but no sign of the pilot.

"It looks like the pilot made it out of the airplane!" Davis announced, drawing cheers from the girls, George, Paula, Grandma Helen, Evelyn's mom, the digging crew, and curious onlookers who had been watching throughout the morning.

"Yay! He made it!" Sandia cheered.

"Yes!" said Evelyn. "Well, maybe. He still had to swim ashore. That is, assuming he belly landed in the water, and not on the actual beach. But..."

Evelyn thought for a moment. She looked very perplexed.

"... If he survived, why hasn't anybody ever heard about this?"

George overheard Evelyn ask this.

"If we can get the tail number from the airplane," said George, "we'll be able to look it up and find out what happened here. And what happened to the pilot."

THE NEXT DAY, EXCAVATION OF THE PLANE RESUMED BRIGHT and early in the morning.

"Hey, everyone..." Ariana said quietly. "Look over there, toward the parking lot. Is that..."

"Sarah Broche!" Treeka hollered. "From Channel 9." Everyone in Portsbury knew who Sarah Broche was. She was a local legend.

The girls raced to meet her. There was a man behind her, carrying a big video camera.

"Hello!" said Ariana.

"You're Sarah Broche—from Channel 9!" Treeka blurted.

"Yes, I am," Sarah Broche replied, chuckling lightly.

"Hi!" Ariana replied. The others stood silent, unsure what to do. It was their job to keep people away from the site. But did "people" include famous local news reporters?

"I heard that a young girl discovered a military plane buried in the sand," said Sarah, pointing to the excavation site with two tail fins and a cockpit sticking out of it. "Was it one of you?"

Evelyn cleared her throat. "Uh, yes, ma'am."

Sarah Broche nodded to the man next to her. He propped his big camera on his shoulder and began recording.

"How did you come to make this miraculous discovery?" Sarah asked, speaking into her microphone, then pointing the microphone toward Evelyn.

"Well, it all started with my latest invention, the Detectorosa 850..." Evelyn began, suddenly grinning ear-to- ear, as she described how she used her metal detector the morning after the big storm.

That evening, everyone it Portsbury—and millions of other people across the country—would be talking about the mysterious P-38 Lightning and the brilliant young girl who found her.

10

MONA

By the third morning, large crowds had formed near the excavation and news crews from all over the country arrived. The small parking lot was full, as hundreds of cars parked anywhere they could in the vicinity and people walked long distances to reach the excavation site.

The spectators had heard about Evelyn and the P-38 on the news. They came from all over—some people even drove hundreds of miles—to witness the plane slowly emerge from the sand.

Today was the day.

The tail assembly, cockpit, and long tail booms that

connected the tail to the wings had been exposed the day before.

At last, at noon, the wings and twin engines were uncovered, too.

This was the big moment people had been waiting for, as everyone celebrated and took lots of pictures, as well as video shots for all the news stations.

Everyone, that is, except for Evelyn.

She was much more interested in something nobody else was talking about—something very important. Something *under* the plane.

But already, the P-38 was a sight to behold. It looked amazing!

George and Grandma Helen stopped by to see the progress that had been made. Davis approached them and the girls.

"This beauty is in remarkably good condition," said Davis. "Especially considering what salt water usually does to steel.

"I'm guessing she was under anaerobic mud or silt for most of these years," he continued. "The steel air frame isn't nearly as corroded as most sea water wrecks from this era. And the plane's aluminum skin almost looks pristine in a few areas!"

"That's great news!" cried George.

"Unfortunately, we couldn't read the tail number," said Davis. "It might be hard to I.D. this bird."

Evelyn was saddened to hear this. She had so many questions!

But just then, as though a magic genie had read Evelyn's mind, a woman called out.

"Hey, Davis! Come quick!"

She had been digging beneath the airplane's nose—the center nacelle, or metal housing, that enclosed the plane's cockpit and guns. Davis and the others rushed over to see what she had found.

And right before their very eyes, they saw black letters—still in excellent condition—hand-painted in cursive script onto the nacelle. The letters spelled the word "Mona."

"Mona!" Davis announced loudly to the whole crew. "Looks like our fine lady has a name!"

The entire crew cheered, for they all knew what this meant. They would now be able to search the records to learn the official history of this aircraft and her pilot.

The news reporters were especially excited. Nothing could make a story about a lost plane more interesting than giving it a name like Mona.

"Hey, Davis," said Paula. "How long before we can pull her out?"

"Give us another twenty-four hours," Davis replied.

"Sounds good. I'll see you tomorrow," Paula announced, as she headed to the parking lot. "I need to go make some phone calls."

BY NOON THE FOLLOWING DAY, THE NEWS CREWS HAD LEFT AND the crowds had thinned out to just a dozen or so spectators.

After all the initial excitement died down, there wasn't much need to guard the perimeter. So, Treeka, Mattie, and Sandia killed time by playing Frisbee.

Ariana was still needed, however, as she continued to meticulously document every step of the excavation in photographs.

But Evelyn just sat there. She sat in the shade of a beach umbrella, watching and waiting, barely moving, for hours. The crew had placed metal structures beneath the plane to support its weight. They then began to dig the sand and mud out from beneath it.

Ariana was not only super perceptive, but she was also Evelyn's best friend. She walked over to Evelyn and sat down.

"You've been watching the exact same spot for hours," Ariana said. "What's up?"

Evelyn smiled. She paused for a long time before speaking.

"The sound of the waves relaxes me," she said.

Ariana nodded, staring out at the rolling surf. "That's called 'alpha' state," she said. "I sometimes listen to a wave machine when I'm painting. It puts me in 'flow mode'—that's when people are most creative."

Evelyn looked away from the plane and turned her gaze toward Ariana.

"For real?" Evelyn asked.

"Yep," said Ariana. "Listening to ocean waves makes your brainwaves slow down. The chatty part of your brain kind of goes to sleep so the creative part can do neat stuff."

"Huh," said Evelyn. "I might have to try that sometime."

"You should totally invent the Brainwaver Flowifier 67,000 or something," said Ariana.

"It crossed my mind," said Evelyn. "But that name is ridiculous."

The two girls laughed.

"But really," said Ariana, more serious. "What's up?"

"I'm waiting to see what's under the airplane," said Evelyn.

"Why?" asked Ariana, looking at the part of the airplane where Evelyn was watching the crew dig.

"Two reasons," said Evelyn. "First, to see whether the landing gear is up or down. I'm assuming the gear is up—meaning the wheels are folded up into tail booms. Because, like I said, the plane probably belly landed in the water. If the gear is down—that would be weird—but it would change the whole story. It would mean our pilot friend landed Mona on the beach, like it was a runway."

"Ok. And the other reason?" asked Ariana.

"To see what he was carrying," said Evelyn. "If anything. There might not be anything there."

"What might he have been carrying?" asked Ariana.

"Bombs, maybe," said Evelyn. "Possibly other stuff."

"What!?" cried Ariana. "Wouldn't that be dangerous?"

"I doubt it, after all these years in the ocean," said Evelyn. "If there's any risk at all, I'm sure they'll clear the area. These folks are experts."

Just then, one of the diggers motioned for Davis to come look at something. Davis crouched down and inspected something beneath the wing. Another member of the crew came over and took a close look. They talked for a moment, and then Davis nodded to the digger, who continued digging.

Davis stood up and got everyone's attention to make an announcement.

"Listen up, please, everybody," Davis said, loudly enough to be heard by everyone.

"Just a quick safety note... we identified a potentially hazardous object beneath the wing, but we have positively confirmed that it's harmless... it's just an external fuel tank. Thanks, that's all."

The crew resumed their work.

"Interesting..." murmured Evelyn.

PAULA CAME RUNNING UP THE BEACH.

"I have an announcement, everyone!" she yelled. She was nearly bursting with excitement. Everyone stopped working and gathered around her.

"I've been on the phone all morning with the Mayor's office and the City Council. There is going to be a public unveiling ceremony!" Paula said.

"Yay!" the girls and the crew all cheered.

"Wait, it gets even better..." said Paula. "The Historic Preservation Commission board has agreed to fund the restoration of this P-38—I mean, Mona."

George and Davis were shocked at this news, and thanked Paula for all of her help.

Evelyn's eyes grew wide. This exceeded her biggest hopes. She might be able to see the P-38 returned to its original form!

"But wait! There's even more!" said Paula.

"The best part!?" she continued, "Mona is going to have a permanent home in the Benson Building on 3rd Street and Willow," Paula continued. "People will come to see it from all over the country!"

"Will Mona be able to fly again?" Evelyn asked eagerly.

"I'm afraid she's been in the water too long to ever fly again," Davis explained.

Evelyn frowned. She had hoped that "restoring" Mona meant "good as new," just like the Glacier Girl P-38 that had been brought up from under the ice in Greenland.

"But she will be cleaned up really well for everyone to see," Davis assured her. "Trust me, she'll be gorgeous."

"We're planning to hold a ceremony to unveil her on October 23rd!" Paula proclaimed.

Evelyn squealed. Her friends all turned to look at her. It was an unusual sound to escape from Evelyn's mouth. She even surprised herself!

Paula looked right at the girls of STEAMTeam 5.

"And you're all invited!"

11

THE GALA

On the evening of October 23rd, a row of reporters' cameras flashed as elegant people dressed in evening gowns and tuxedos walked up a red carpet into the lobby of the Benson Building, off 3rd Street and Willow.

Hundreds of people had come to see the grand unveiling of Mona, the restored P-38 Lightning that lay hidden for seventy years under the sand and waves off the coast, next to their quiet little town.

The members of STEAMTeam 5 and their parents arrived. That is, except for Evelyn. She and her family had not yet arrived.

"Where's Evelyn?" Ariana asked. "She's never late!"

Sandia, Treeka, and Mattie just shrugged. They had never known Evelyn to ever be late, for anything.

Paula Youngblood approached the girls.

"Hi girls! Don't you all look pretty!" she said, with a giant smile. The girls did not usually wear dresses, but this was a special occasion.

"Have you seen Evelyn?" Paula asked, looking a little worried. The event was about to begin, and Evelyn was not only a guest of honor for discovering the plane, but she had become a local celebrity as well.

Just then, Paula and the girls all saw a burgundy SUV screech to a stop in front of the red carpet. Evelyn's parents, Grandma Helen, and George Lee all got out. George straightened his bow tie and offered his arm for Grandma Helen. "Okay," she said, taking his arm. "But just for backup."

"Where's Evelyn?" asked Sandia. The girls all looked back at the SUV.

A fancy blue shoe extended from the darkness inside the SUV. Evelyn stepped out, wearing a dark blue gown. Her hair was up. She looked beautiful.

The girls all gasped!

"Wowwww!" said all the girls.

"What happened to your... ponytail?" asked Mattie. The girls had never seen Evelyn without her ponytail, and her trademark blue, pink, and yellow 3-ball ponytail holder.

Evelyn walked gracefully up the carpet. She was stone-faced, but then winked at her friends as she held up her wrist, revealing that she was wearing her blue, pink, and yellow ponytail holder as a bracelet. Then she busted out laughing and all the girls hugged.

"Oh good, you made it!" said Paula. "Evelyn, if you'll please come with me, I'll show you your seat and walk you through the program. Excuse us, girls," Paula said to the others. Evelyn just smiled and shrugged to her friends as she departed with Paula.

The girls walked over to George, Grandma Helen, and Davis James. They were talking to an elderly woman in a fancy evening gown. Her name was Dorothy Benson.

Everyone in Portsbury knew who Mrs. Benson was. She supported the local arts and charities, and she had donated the old manufacturing building to the city a few years before. Everyone in town was excited about its re-opening as the permanent home of Mona, the P-38 Lightning.

"Jim would have loved knowing they were restoring an old fighter plane in his building," Mrs. Benson said.

A car pulled up in front of the building and stopped. An old man stepped out and looked around. Two women climbed out of the car and each extended an arm. The man reached out to hold onto them both. He appeared fragile but somehow still quite strong.

"You okay, dad?" one of the women asked.

"I'm good," the old man replied.

Together, they entered the building to join the others. There must have been about 300 people there. A string quartet played music in the background.

Paula saw the old man and rushed over to greet him.

"You must be Lieutenant Charles McCullen," she said, gushing somewhat as she extended her hand to shake his.

"Good evening, everyone!" said Davis James, his voice booming over the microphone. He stood up on the stage. "I led this little warbird recovery project."

The crowd filled the room with applause.

"Please take your seats up at the front—we have some seats reserved," Paula told Lieutenant McCullen and his family. The other seats filled up, with many more people standing to the sides and in the back. The room started to quiet down.

Paula joined Davis on the stage. "Many of you know the woman who made tonight's gala event possible," said Davis. "Please say hello to Paula Youngblood."

The crowd applauded again.

"We'd like to introduce you all to... Mona!" Paula announced as the area behind the stage lit up. A satin drape was hoisted up, revealing the restored P-38 Lightning.

The crowd went wild! There were gasps and applause and even some whistles as they admired the stunning sight before them. Mona's beauty was unquestionable. The old plane sparkled under the bright lights. It was separated from the crowd by a big, yellow, satin ribbon.

"As beautiful as ever," Lieutenant Charles McCullen said, barely above a whisper. His daughter reached out to hold his hand, and he patted it softly.

When the room quieted, Paula began to speak. "I'd like to introduce you all to Portsbury's new media darling, the amazing young woman who found this airplane, using a metal detector that she built herself!"

The crowd went wild again! People clapped and clapped.

"Evelyn, please stand up!" said Paula.

Evelyn stood up and waved to everybody, blushing a bit at all of the attention. Camera flashes made the whole room sparkle like diamonds.

"But wait, there's more," Paula said, chuckling into the microphone. "We have another special guest tonight... I think we've managed to keep it a secret until this moment."

The crowd went silent. Who could it be?

Paula continued. "Please welcome Lieutenant Charles McCullen, Mona's pilot!"

The crowd gasped... they had not seen this coming. They cheered as he made his way up to the stage. Evelyn gasped, too! The plane had been flown by this man! Not only had he survived the crash, but he was still alive after all these years!

Paula motioned him over to the podium and adjusted the microphone for him. The crowd sat down again. He leaned forward to speak.

"Thank you, everyone. Thank you," he said. "It is truly an honor to be here, and it's my dream to be reunited with my first love... Mona."

The crowd stood up and cheered again. He waved at them to take a seat.

"It's an honor to be here and to be asked to cut the ribbon to commemorate this great restoration project..." he continued.

"I flew Mona with the 343rd fighter group from 1942 to 1945," Lieutenant McCullen explained. "It was during the second world war, and she was one of the most fearsome birds in the sky." The audience applauded. He paused to smile, reflecting on his memories of days long past.

He cleared his throat before continuing. "It was May 25, 1945, I was patrolling for enemy submarines off the coast, when I lost her to the sea," he said. Everyone in the audience grew quiet.

Lieutenant McCullen turned around to face Mona. He reached his hand out to touch the tip of her newly polished nose.

"Or, I thought I lost her," he said quietly. Then he turned to face the audience again.

"There was a terrible storm—not unlike the one the night before Mona was found..."

"I had been flying all night..." he said. "I was only seven miles out when the weather turned ugly."

His voice filled with anxiety. "I didn't have enough fuel to go around the storm, so I decided to fly through it. But lightning hit my starboard engine and it caught fire."

"I bailed out. I climbed out onto the wing and jumped off, a few hundred yards from the shore," he said with a long sigh.

"I never thought I'd see her again," Lieutenant McCullen continued. "Until you called me and asked me to unveil her today," he added, looking over toward Paula.

"And this project would never have come to be if it hadn't been for a smart, curious young woman," he said.

"So, I'd like to ask that young woman to lend me a hand."

"Can I ask Evelyn, the young engineer who discovered Mona on the beach, to please come up on stage and help me cut the ribbon?"

This caught Evelyn off guard. Her mind had been someplace else. Something the Lieutenant had said didn't make sense.

Evelyn suddenly realized everybody was looking at her.

"Go ahead," Evelyn's mother said with a nod. Her father smiled proudly.

Her friends cheered loudly as Evelyn regained herself and stepped up onto the stage next to the Lieutenant. He reached out his hand to shake hers. Evelyn was so excited that her heart was racing.

"Good work!" he told her. "This is your treasure, too."

Paula handed them a huge pair of scissors.

"Shall we?" the lieutenant asked Evelyn as he turned to face Mona. Evelyn smiled and nodded enthusiastically.

Together, they cut the ribbon, and the crowd exploded into cheers.

Sarah Broche, the local news reporter, appeared from nowhere and stuck her microphone between the two of them. "How does it feel to meet the man who flew this plane so many years ago?" she asked Evelyn.

"Amazing," said Evelyn, a bit taken aback.

"And you, sir, how does it feel to be reunited with your long lost love, Mona?" Sarah said, pointing her microphone at the Lieutenant.

"Tonight's the best night of my life!" said Lieutenant McCullen.

Sarah turned back to Evelyn. "What's next for you? Any new inventions we should know about? Any more treasure hunts you've got planned?"

"Well, yes, actually," Evelyn said. "I've been thinking about waterproofing my metal detector so I can take it scuba diving."

"Impressive young lady," Sarah Broche said into the camera. She then turned to get comments from Paula Youngblood and Davis James.

Evelyn fixed her eyes on the Lieutenant. Something didn't add up. In all the noise and commotion, she slowly backed away from the crowd, pretending to look at other parts of the airplane.

She discreetly pulled out her phone and started tapping its screen, occasionally looking up to make sure no one was watching.

12

SECRETS

"*E*velyn!" shouted Sandia, startling Evelyn. "There you are!"

The girls had been looking all over for her in the crowd. They walked over to Evelyn, who quickly put away her phone.

"Why are you hiding behind an airplane wheel?" asked Treeka.

"Landing gear," said Evelyn.

"Landing gear," said Treeka.

"Um, I was just..." Evelyn stammered. "Can you excuse me please? I'll be right back!"

Evelyn disappeared into the crowd. The girls were curious, but they soon became distracted by all of the intricate details of the airplane, which had been cleaned up and polished quite remarkably since they had last seen it, all muddy and banged up on the beach.

Evelyn made her way through the crowd to Lieutenant McCullen.

"Excuse me, sir," she said to the Lieutenant. "Would you mind if I asked you a question?"

"Of course, ask anything you like," the Lieutenant said, curious.

Evelyn motioned for him to step away from the people near him. It was clear that she would prefer they didn't hear. He understood and looked concerned.

"What is it?" he asked. "Is everything okay?"

Evelyn bit her lip, not wanting to say anything inappropriate. But she just had to know the truth.

"Well, three things, actually" she said.

"Number one. You said you were patrolling the coast for submarines. But the 343rd was based out of the Aleutian Islands in Alaska. We found Mona with external fuel tanks under the wings, which are only used for long-range missions. You were over 2,800 miles from home, sir. Much too far from home to be on a routine sub patrol."

Lieutenant McCullen raised his eyebrows.

"Number two," Evelyn continued. "Your plane could not have been hit by lightning. I just checked with the national weather archive. On May 25, 1945, the sky was clear at Flint Falls Airfield, with zero precipitation and a 5 mile per hour wind from the west. There wouldn't be a storm in this area for another three weeks."

The Lieutenant raised his eyebrows even higher.

"Number three. It's impossible to bail out of a P-38 by jumping off the wing. The tail assembly would cut you in half. There are two ways to bail out of a Lightning: You either slide headfirst down the trailing edge of the wing, or you turn the plane upside down, open the canopy, release your seatbelt, and drop out."

"Remarkable," said the Lieutenant.

Evelyn shrugged. "I like airplanes."

"I can see that," he said.

The Lieutenant thought long and hard, as though wrestling with himself in his mind. At last, he spoke.

"Can you keep a secret?" he asked her.

"Oh boy, can I ever," Evelyn said. She instantly realized that might have been saying too much. She was thinking about the giant secret she keeps every minute of every day, about STEAMTeam 5's top-secret Makerspace located beneath Shell Mountain.

"Between you and me," the Lieutenant whispered, "I lied up there on stage."

"I know," said Evelyn. "I'm just wondering why."

"For national security," he said. "Follow me." The Lieutenant guided Evelyn to Mona's tail fin so they could speak more privately.

"I don't know if I should be telling you this," he said, looking a little nervous. Then he chuckled. "But what are they gonna do? I'm 96 years old."

Evelyn smiled. *"Who are 'they'?"* she thought to herself.

"I think you've earned the right to know the truth," he said. "You are right. I didn't bail out in any storm."

Evelyn's eyes opened wide.

"I was on a secret mission. I was a courier, transporting something very, VERY important."

This time, it was Evelyn who raised her eyebrows.

"I had just flown through the night, almost 1800 miles, after refueling at Fort Randall in Alaska. And when I was only a few miles from landing at Flint Falls, the strangest thing happened."

The lieutenant's gaze intensified as he looked straight into Evelyn's eyes.

"I received an encrypted, top-secret order to ditch my plane and the item I was carrying."

Evelyn squinted. "That sounds... odd," she said. "Didn't you think it was a strange order?"

"Oh yes!" he said. "I had never heard of anything like that ever happening."

"What were you transporting?" Evelyn inquired.

"It was a black box. With a handle on it. About this big," he said, holding up his hands to the size of a loaf of bread.

"I don't know what was in the box. I never found out," he said.

"What did you do!?" asked Evelyn. "I would have been terrified. I mean, to ditch a perfectly good—and rather expensive—airplane in the ocean, not to mention risking your life, when you had a perfectly good airfield just minutes away!"

The lieutenant laughed.

"You're tellin' me!" he said. "I don't even like swimming in a swimming pool. So forget the ocean. Fish scare me."

"But," he continued, "I knew there had to be a good reason. I knew it was important that nobody find that black box. So important, that the army wanted the world to think that I'd been lost at sea, for a while anyway."

"So did you belly land the plane on the water?"

The lieutenant smiled.

"Yes," he said. "I did actually jump off the wing. But after I landed and the plane was starting to sink."

Then he looked around to make sure no one was listening, and he leaned in to whisper.

"But the black box was not inside of it!"

Evelyn was shocked. But then she thought about it.

"Of course!" she realized. "We didn't find any box inside Mona's cockpit."

"You see," he continued, "I figured that if that box was so darn important that they'd want me to waste a P-38, then they really didn't want it to get found. I figured somebody might locate the airplane where I set her down in shallow water."

Evelyn nodded.

"So before I landed, I threw the box out the canopy. Dropped it right into the ocean!"

Evelyn's jaw dropped at this.

"And do you wanna know the best part?" he said, his serious expression suddenly breaking into a wide grin.

Evelyn nodded eagerly.

"I know exactly where it is!"

"Where?!" asked Evelyn.

"I dropped it into the water right next to one of the boulders out by the Otter Point lighthouse."

"That's incredible!" said Evelyn. "We drive by that lighthouse all the time! Did you ever go look for it?"

"No, I never got the chance to return to search for it. I was back on Attu Island in a month, with a new airplane. The war ended a few months later, and I went home to New Jersey, started a family."

"For years," he continued, "I thought it best to leave it at the bottom of the ocean. "

Evelyn nodded.

"But so much time has passed, I reckon it couldn't do any harm now. But... I never had the skills or the right equipment. Remember, I don't like the ocean."

"Ah, right," said Evelyn. "Fish."

"Fish," said the lieutenant with a nod.

"Now, didn't I hear you tell that reporter something about scuba diving?"

"Yeeeess... " said Evelyn cautiously, not quite sure where this was going.

He smiled and she saw a twinkle in his eye.

"Are you saying?..." she began.

"You can't tell a soul!" he said. "At least, not until we know what's inside the box."

"What about my friends?" Evelyn asked. "They help me with stuff like this. We're a team. And believe me, they can keep gigantic secrets."

The lieutenant understood. He respected Evelyn's loyalty and her faith in her friends.

"When the time is right," he said. "But for now, it's our secret, okay?

Evelyn nodded. "I promise."

Lieutenant McCullen looked up and noticed that Davis, Paula, and a group of people were beginning to approach them. The other STEAMTeam 5 girls were with them, too.

Davis James bellowed over the crowd. "Don't be shy!" he commanded, waving Evelyn and Lieutenant McCullen to the stage. "This is your moment!"

"Let's go take some pictures," Lieutenant McCullen said to Evelyn. As they walked, he turned to whisper in her ear. "Welcome to the mission, Evelyn."

The End

COMING SOON:

STEAMTeam 5 Chronicles: Evelyn Engineer and the Black Box at Otter Point

FREE EBOOK

To receive a free .PDF of *STEAMTeam 5 Chronicles: Mystery of the Haunted Cider Mill*, send an email to:

info@steamteam5.com

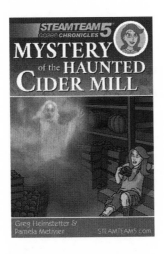

Made in the USA
Middletown, DE
07 October 2020